To every curious youngster who knows that thinking
they know is knowing they don't know... I think.
S. N.

For Bianca, an animal that definitely exists!
J.-B. D.

**Animals That Might Exist by Professor O'Logist**
Text copyright © 2020 by Stéphane Nicolet
Ilustration copyright © 2020 by Jean-Baptiste Drouot
First edition copyright © 2020 Comme des géants

All rights reserved

Editorial and art direction by Nadine Robert
Translation by Mireille Messier
Book design by Jolin Masson

The illustrations of this book were made with ink and watercolors.

This edition published in 2021 by Milky Way Picture Books,
an imprint of Comme des géants inc. Varennes, Quebec, Canada.

Library and Archives Canada Cataloguing in Publication

Title: Animals that might exist, by professor O'Logist / Stéphane Nicolet;
illustrations, Jean-Baptiste Drouot.
Other titles: Animaux qui existent peut-être, du professeur O'Logh. English
Names: Nicolet, Stéphane, 1973- author. | Drouot, Jean-Baptiste, illustrator.
Description: Translation of: Les animaux qui existent peut-être, du professeur O'Logh.
Identifiers: Canadiana 2021004246X | ISBN 9781990252051 (hardcover)
Classification: LCC PS8627.I256 A6213 2022 | DDC jC843/.6—dc23
ISBN: 978-1-990252-05-1

Printed and bound in China

**Milky Way Picture Books**
38 Sainte-Anne Street
Varennes, QC J3X 1R5
Canada

www.milkywaypicturebooks.com

# ANIMALS
## THAT MIGHT EXIST
### by Professor O'Logist

Stéphane Nicolet                    Jean-Baptiste Drouot

Translated by Mireille Messier

Milky Way
Picture Books

# EDITOR'S NOTE

In this animal book, like in most animal books, there are animals. Each one has been carefully studied, detailed, drawn, and classified by Professor O'Logist, a little-known scientist and orphan from birth. This rare volume of work has been carefully edited using the notes in the professor's notebook. We found his journal in the depths of a jungle, home to the Korowai people (as opposed to the professor himself, who was nowhere to be found).

There are only 78 copies of this publication in the world. The creatures featured in this book are so incredible that the professor had to invent a new and entirely revolutionary classification system. So revolutionary, in fact, that the Royal Society of Zoology rejected it and banned the poor man, calling him a "miserable kook" and a "fibber" (neither of which are very royal nor scientific). None of these animals have been observed since, which isn't to say they don't exist, as some have suggested. No one has ever proven that they don't exist, at least.

The following is a transcription of the first page of the journal, which was found badly damaged.

*I like pets, but not in my home.*

– Professor O'Logist


*Dear unknown reader,*

*I'm not sure how you found my journal, nor when you plan to read it.
But it all started like this: one day, having grown tired of my dear, old,
rainy England, with her white sheep and dreary, grey snails, I set off
to explore the world to find new, yet-to-be-discovered (and preferably
extraordinary) exotic animals.*

*On my poor mother's head, I swear to you that I found every single one
of these animals. They are all here in my trusty notebook. I can only hope,
dear future reader, that my life's work has since been recognized and that
the scientific community is finally ready to accept it — because the world
deserves to know.*

*Kisses,*

– Arturo

# TABLE OF CONTENTS

# 1

The Soft
Animals

PLATE I

# THE
# GLOOBEECEPHALUS

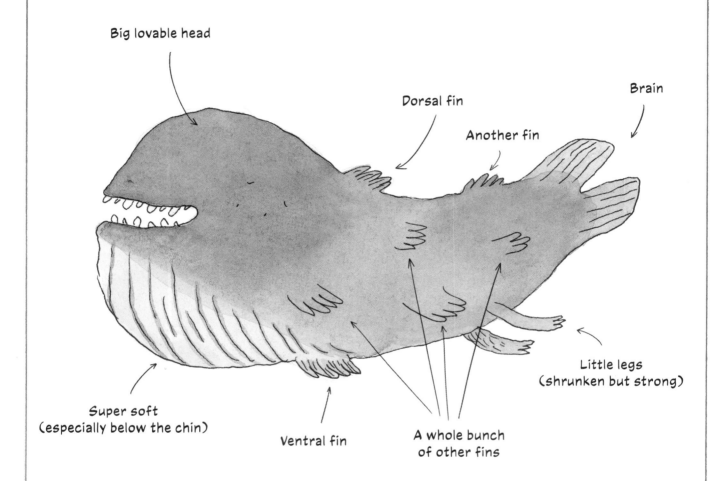

Big lovable head

Dorsal fin

Another fin

Brain

Little legs
(shrunken but strong)

A whole bunch
of other fins

Ventral fin

Super soft
(especially below the chin)

**DISTINGUISHING FEATURES**
Loves smoked sausages.

Its call, known as "vroomining," can't be heard by humans and that's a good thing…

The more it eats, the softer it gets.

**LENGTH**
6 m / 20 ft

**HABITAT**
Mariana Trench, Guam

PLATE II

According to the Indigenous peoples of the area, the gloobeecephalus (or grachaloo) is quite the glutton, as it must ingest several tons of food per day. That's when its many fins and little legs come in handy: it can retrieve its nourishment all the way down at the bottom of an abyss or, more simply, from a hot-dog stand. Despite its enormous head, the gloobeecephalus is a wee bit daft given its stomach is in its skull and its brain is… well, elsewhere. Much lower. It is also covered in velvety skin, which serves no purpose since it has never been touched.

It is very, very, very* rare to observe the gloobeecephalus in its natural habitat. In fact, it is likely feasting on albino calamari from the depths of the ocean as you read this.

*Fig. 1* GLOOBEECEPHALUS HUNTING 253 CHEESY HOT DOGS

* Did I mention how rare it is? It's very rare!

PLATE III

# THE
# FLAMINGHOUND

Long, short-haired ears

Litter of 3-4 pups

Fur as soft as
a hipster's beard

Hairless legs

Specimen getting
ready to sleep

Inverted knees
(wobbly balance)

Tail: 80 cm / 31.5 in

Long, long-haired tail

**DISTINGUISHING FEATURES**
Carries its young on its back until
they can run on their own legs.

Insulation properties: R-30

**WEIGHT**
12 kg (9 of which are fur)

26 lb (20 of which are fur)

**LENGTH**
2 m / 6.5 ft

**HABITAT**
Salar de Uyuni, Bolivia

PLATE IV

This strange animal has the grace of a pink flamingo and the hairiness of a greyhound. Sometimes, as the sun sets and the dusk falls on the salt marshes, one can marvel as it sleeps on three legs despite its lack of balance. It would be much better off sleeping on a couch, but that would leave the furniture covered in pink fur. Of course, this possibility would never occur to the flaminghound, as it is not the most intelligent of animals. For example, if you throw a ball for it to fetch, it will run without stopping and never come back (except certain specimens with exceptional stamina that will run right around the planet and return to their initial spot). Because its fur is highly sought after, the flaminghound is considered an endangered species.

It is fascinating to observe these animals chirping in the salt desert. One can only wonder what they are talking about…

*Fig. 1* **A FLOCK OF FLAMINGHOUNDS TRYING TO IMPRESS VISITORS**

PLATE V

# THE
# SNËEAK

Sheep wool

Sheep tail

Sheep head

BÄÄÄÄwwwhhhh!

Sheep bleat

Sheep legs

Sheep smell

**DISTINGUISHING FEATURE**
The only difference between a snëeak and a real sheep is that its wool can be washed in hot water without shrinking.*

**WIDTH**
80 cm / 31.5 in

**HABITAT**
Finland's Kaakkurivaara region

* One must still find it, fleece it, and know how to knit.

PLATE VI

The deceptively cute, entirely horrible snëeak is a soft, wooly predator that feeds on the fleece of living sheep. Some refer to it as a "knitomaniac." It looks like a regular sheep in every respect except for its razor-sharp jaw similar to titanium, self-sharpening, double-bladed shears. In the Finnish countryside, where the snëeak lives, it is not unusual to see entire flocks of shivering, naked sheep. (Though it is worth noting that even sheep with their wool still shiver a little bit in that part of the country.) While it's impossible to observe this master of mimicry in action, if one listens carefully, it is possible to hear the snëeak bleating ominously from the center of an unsuspecting flock about to be fleeced. The snëeak usually hunts alone to avoid confusion.

*Fig. 1* TWO SPECIMENS ATTEMPTING TO BE PACK HUNTERS

PLATE VII

# THE
# FRINGEODON
# CARPETUS

Floppy fins,
always odd-numbered

Varied shape, depending
on water temperature

Hairless face

Eyes
Nostrils

Nostrils
Eyes

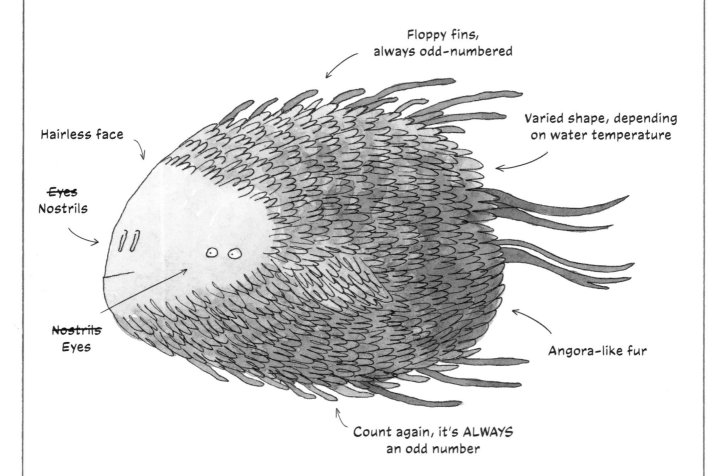

Angora-like fur

Count again, it's ALWAYS
an odd number

**DISTINGUISHING FEATURES**
It's really hard to tell the nostrils
and eyes apart.

When raised in cold water, it
may become triangular, but never
isosceles.

**RADIUS**
1.5 m / 5 ft

**DIAMETER**
3 m / 10 ft

**PERIMETER**
9.42 m / 30.9 ft

**AREA**
7.7 m² / 25.3 ft²

**HABITAT**
Northern beaches of Madagascar

PLATE VIII

The Fringeodon Carpetus is commonly known as the "rug fish." According to the Indigenous peoples of the area, the specimen seen here is believed to be a baby, as adults can grow up to a diameter of 2–3 meters (6.5–10 ft). This fish lives at the bottom of the ocean, which explains why it is bare on one side and has its eyes and nostrils on the other. Because it is very flat and furry, it transforms easily into a gorgeous carpet when dried. The Fringeodon Carpetus is completely harmless and somewhat curious, which likely explains why it is now extinct. After all, who doesn't love a nice carpet?

But beware! There are similar-looking species who behave in a very aggressive manner. These counterfeits, often hastily dried, have flooded the international market.

*Fig. 1* DEVASTATION CAUSED BY A COUNTERFEIT

# The Drooly
# Animals

PLATE IX

# THE
# BOUFFANDACTYL

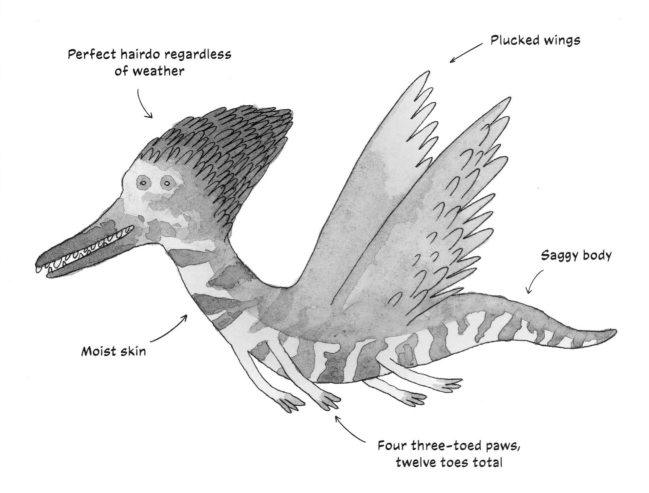

Perfect hairdo regardless
of weather

Plucked wings

Saggy body

Moist skin

Four three-toed paws,
twelve toes total

**DISTINGUISHING FEATURES**
Feeds exclusively on cheese and
fermented fish juice (*nuoc-mâm*).

Can count to twelve.

**WINGSPAN**
Approx. 1.6308654 m /
5.3506083 ft

**HABITAT**
Ireland, near cheese factories

PLATE X

The bouffandactyl, known for its remarkable hairstyle, is afflicted with unbearable halitosis. Despite being somewhat repulsive, though, it makes for great company. Loyal to a fault and a bit on the mischievous side, it could easily dethrone the dog for the title of "man's best friend."

Regrettably, it tends to be a spitter, which explains why it never graduated to the ranks of other companion animals. As a result of this misfortune, the bouffandactyl has made itself scarce. It is easy to track, as it leaves behind a strange, lingering smell of cheese and shea hairspray.

Some enthusiasts have tried to breed bouffandactyls, but the equipment required has proven too cumbersome. Abandonment is also common among them.

*Fig. 1* AN UNFORTUNATE OUTCOME OF AMATEUR BREEDING

PLATE XI

# THE
# SILVERBACK
# ACHOOLUG

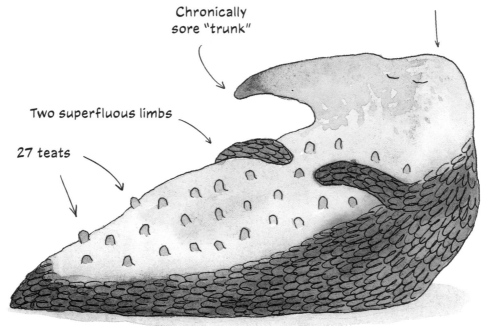

Concentrating on its nap

Chronically
sore "trunk"

Two superfluous limbs

27 teats

Large slug-like
creature with scales

**DISTINGUISHING FEATURE**
Nothing

**LENGTH FULLY STRETCHED**
18 cm / 7 in

**HABITAT**
Anywhere in the world
under the right conditions

PLATE XII

This impressive creature lives luxuriously reclined in puddles, even in places like deserts or underground parking lots. Given the serious lack of puddles in these locations, however, it creates its own puddles by filling holes with its saliva (or "drool," for all the bodily fluid beginners out there). This species is strictly composed of females, made obvious by their 27 teats. These mammaries serve no purpose given there are no males and, therefore, no babies. Still, the population remains stable, which suggests that the silverback achoolug are immortal. It is unfortunate to be both eternal and completely useless, but there you have it.

Upon closer investigation, it's not drool; it's snot. This would explain the achoolug's red snout and the hair-raising sneezes heard throughout the night in the deserts and underground parking lots.

*Fig. 1* ACHOOLUG ATTEMPTING TO COUNT ITS TEATS

# The Supernatural
# Animals

PLATE XIII

# THE
# MOOT

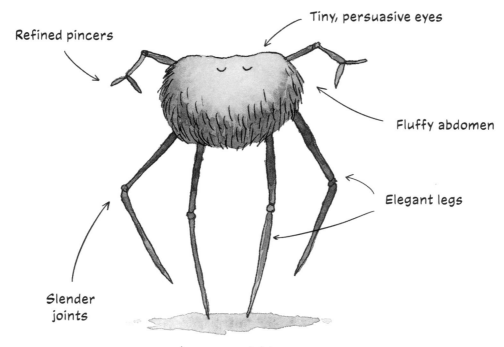

Refined pincers

Tiny, persuasive eyes

Fluffy abdomen

Elegant legs

Slender joints

Average weight:
45.53 kg / 96 lb

Color according to cooking time
(at 75°C or 167°F)

Raw     5 min     7 min     10 min

**DISTINGUISHING FEATURES**

Changes color when cooked.

Rolls up in the shape of a retro footstool in case of danger.

Eats precious metals.

**STANDING HEIGHT**
1.93 m / 6.33 ft

**HABITAT**
Kwamalasamutu Forest (I forget which country this was in…)

PLATE XIV

This slight animal is considered a deity by local Indigeneous peoples and feeds exclusively on their offerings. In return, they ask it questions and the moot replies by performing strange movements with its long legs, which are then interpreted by the locals. The moot is never wrong! However, it can only guess the present: for example, if it's nice outside and one asks it if it's nice outside, after three hours of gesticulary meditation, it answers "yes." At least, that's what the locals claim.

It is difficult to know more about the moot because the locals do not like explorers to go near it.

*Fig. 1* MOOT DURING A DIVINATION SESSION

PLATE XV

# THE
# POTTOS-TATTOS

Underwhelming mane

Ear (unless it's on
the other side...)

Spotted fur
(males only)

Happy little grin

Inverted hind legs

**DISTINGUISHING FEATURES**
Only has one ear, which
is unobservable.

Understands all Belgian dialects.

**HEIGHT**
7 cm / 2.8 in

**DEPTH**
3 m / 9.8 ft

**LENGTH**
17 cm / 6.7 in

**WIDTH**
7 cm / 2.8 in

**HABITAT**
Agricultural plains
of Northern Europe

PLATE XVI

The pottos-tattos is the only representative of the lemur family in Europe. No bigger than a guinea pig, it is easily captured due to its inverted hind legs, which force it to walk very slowly, but also give it a rather funny strut that is hard not to poke fun at. Luckily, the pottos-tattos is not easily offended and also likes a good joke. Very popular for its ability to fry potatoes with its mind*, it is easy to feed in that it loves sautéed, mashed, boiled, baked, matchstick, fried, and even scalloped potatoes. Regrettably, there are no pottos-tattos left in the wild as a result of trafficking by fast-food restaurants and snack bars. A trial reinsertion of one pair of pottos-tattos into their natural habitat is currently being tested against the advice of potato farmers, who fear their crop will only yield puffed potatoes.

*Fig. 1* FIRST PAIR OF POTTOS-TATTOS RELEASED INTO A POTATO FIELD

* Known as "chipokinesis".

PLATE XVII

# THE
# VELCROPTUS
# VIBRISSA
# (A.K.A. VV)

Colors ranging from
"winterfresh" blue
to "spearmint" green

Bristles ranging from
"soft" to "hard"

Retractable legs
in case of stress

Gallbladder filled
with fluoride

Minty skin

**DISTINGUISHING FEATURES**
Always chilly.

Free of parabens and titanium
dioxide.

Feeds on tartar.

**LENGTH**
7 cm / 2.7 in

**HABITAT**
At the foot of the
Popocatépetl volcano

PLATE **XVIII**

Despite its size, this minuscule reptile is a direct descendant of the velcrociraptor, an enormous dinosaur. Like its ancestor, it is completely covered in velcro, which allows it to adhere to materials upon which it is flung. Nowadays, this incredible ability is completely useless, but it was also quite pointless in dinosaur times, when no one had the physical strength to throw a velcrociraptor onto fabric (which, in any case, did not yet exist). The true power of the velcroptus vibrissa is its ability to dry instantly when wet. This supernatural talent also contributed to its demise, given that primitive tribes used the VV to brush their teeth by putting the animal on a stick. How wonderful to have a toothbrush that dries in seconds, especially in a rainforest renowned for its humid climate?

It's no coincidence that the primitive language of a primitive tribe in a primitive forest did not have a word for "dentist."

*Fig. 1* **BEDTIME IN THE PRIMITIVE FOREST**

# The Off-key
# Animals

PLATE XIX

# THE
# EARWORMITO

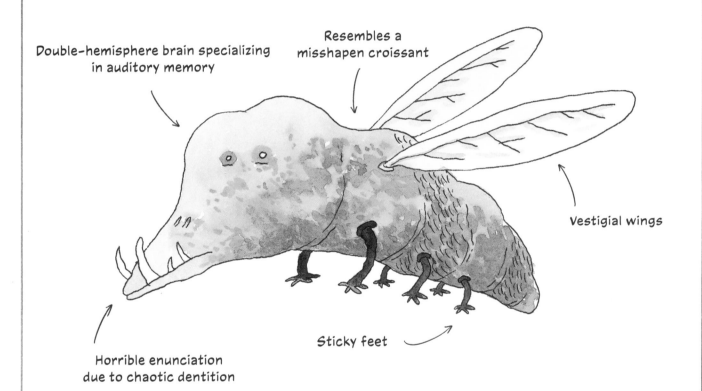

Double-hemisphere brain specializing
in auditory memory

Resembles a
misshapen croissant

Vestigial wings

Horrible enunciation
due to chaotic dentition

Sticky feet

**DISTINGUISHING FEATURES**
Loves songs from the '80s and
the radio in general.

Loves the company of DJs and Jays
with a special penchant for DJs
named Jay.

**LENGTH**
2 cm / 0.8 in

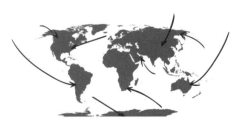

**HABITAT**
Everywhere (practically)

PLATE XX

The earwormito is a nasty insect. Nocturnal, it spends its nights squeaking horrible little songs into your ear with its obnoxious, whiny, tin-rattle voice. These annoying ditties become stuck in your head for the rest of the day and spread to your surroundings by way of uncontrollable humming. Despite its clumsy physique, short legs, and ridiculous wings, the earwormito is surprisingly fast, making it impossible to squish on a wall with a slipper, a book, or a ham. It has no known predators and researchers have yet to find a way to eradicate this insect responsible for the planet's greatest musical pandemics. Worse still, it has the memory of a snuroboros (see plates XLV and XLVI) and has a repertoire of hundreds of irritating songs. Like a music streaming service with wings.*
The only place where the earwormito does not thrive is in northern Yakutia — a scientific anomaly, since this insect is undeterred by the cold and can easily survive in -60°C (-76°F).

*Fig. 1* **THE HARSH CLIMATE FORCES THE YAKUTIANS TO SLEEP WITH TRAPPER HATS COVERING THEIR EARS.**

* *Pestify*

PLATE **XXI**

# THE
# CASTINNITUS

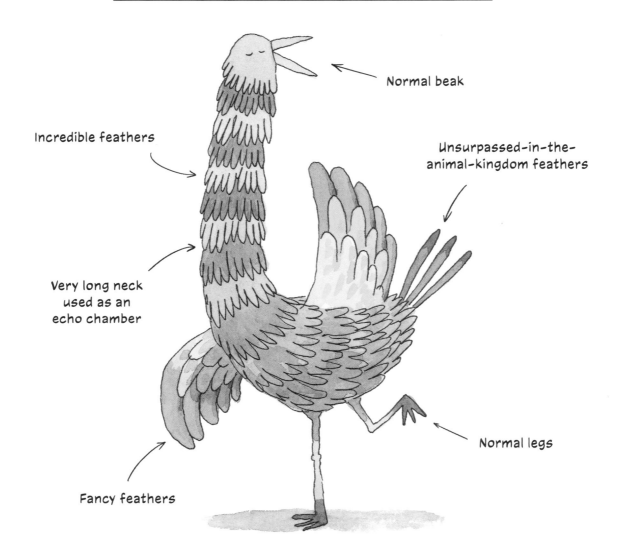

Normal beak

Incredible feathers

Unsurpassed-in-the-animal-kingdom feathers

Very long neck used as an echo chamber

Normal legs

Fancy feathers

**DISTINGUISHING FEATURES**
Color unique to each specimen.

The Chinese call it the Yôuyôuyôy (有有有), which means "Ow ow ow."

Lives up to 23 years.

**HEIGHT**
64 cm (52 of which are neck)

2 ft (1.6 of which are neck)

**HABITAT**
The mountains of Zhangjiajie National Park

PLATE XXII

This bird from the guinea fowl family has a unique plumage: every one of its feathers is striped, iridescent, shimmering, lustrous, golden, glittery, and glitzy. Its flesh is appetizingly moist, easy to chew, naturally savory, and seasoned to perfection. And yet, the Castinnitus is not hunted by humans for one simple reason: this eccentric, oviparous beast is capable of singing with a very, very unpleasant voice at ear-shattering levels of at least 80 decibels. The sound resembles that of a chalk on a chalkboard or a knife scraping a plate. Approaching it without ear protection is the equivalent of chewing on aluminum foil or putting hot peppers under one's eyelids.*

The region's Indigenous population has found a clever solution to the castinnitus: fashioning ear plugs using a small land mollusk** that feeds on umaneerwax (also known as "human earwax" or "ear crud"). This wonderful symbiosis is further proof of nature's ingenuity.

*Fig. 1* ANOTHER QUIET DAY IN ZHANGJIAJIE

* Do not attempt without medical supervision.

** See plate XXXII.

PLATE XXIII

# THE
# CHOTHAWP

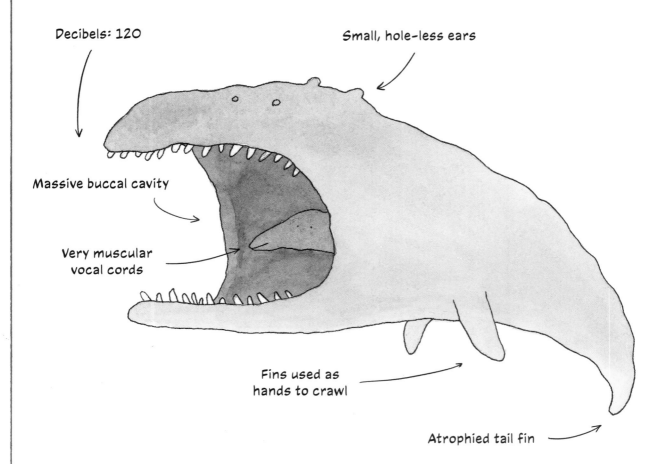

Decibels: 120

Small, hole-less ears

Massive buccal cavity

Very muscular
vocal cords

Fins used as
hands to crawl

Atrophied tail fin

**DISTINGUISHING FEATURES**

Crawls at the bottom of lakes.

Houses a fish in its throat by way
of its vocal cords. Sometimes, the
fish gets accidentally swallowed,
which gives everyone a much-
needed break.

**LENGTH**
Enormous

**WIDTH**
Enormous

**HABITAT**
The deepest lakes of Scotland

PLATE **XXIV**

This cetacean is quite simply unbearable. It sings the same annoying and repetitive song all day, every day. The lyrics are complete nonsense and the melody is grating. It is the height of tedium! The chothawp is detested by all except very young fish. This is because the eardrums of the very young, be they fish or human, are not yet fully formed. They are, therefore, completely tone-deaf to bad music or simple commands like "finish your algae" or "stop spitting on your sister." Fortunately, the chothawp lives at the very bottom of the abyss, meaning that its song is seldom heard above the surface.

*Fig. 1* CHOTHAWP SINGING A TEDIOUS TUNE TO A SHOAL OF TUNA

# The Disgusting Animals

PLATE **XXV**

# THE
# CUCUMBERSOME

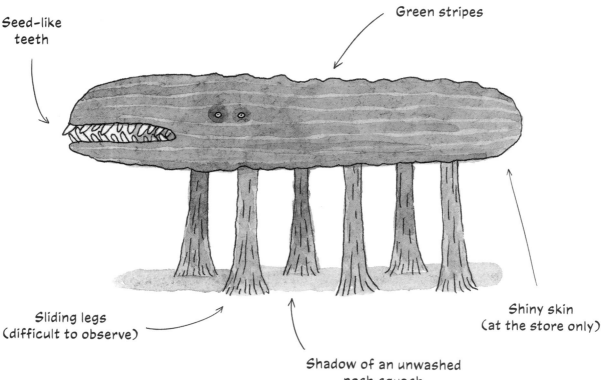

Seed-like teeth

Green stripes

Sliding legs
(difficult to observe)

Shadow of an unwashed
posh squash

Shiny skin
(at the store only)

**DISTINGUISHING FEATURES**
Comprised of 96% water, this is an
aqueous animal.

Its sense of humour is very dry.

It balances out!

**LENGTH**
30 cm / 11.8 in
(same as a cucumber, really!)

**HABITAT**
The crisper drawer

PLATE XXVI

Looking deceptively like a vegetable, with its phony Cucurbitaceae family resemblance, this animal is nothing short of repulsive. It selects a random human and follows it around for days, eating anything that it sheds: dead skin, nail clippings, hair, filth of all sorts… The cucumbersome tends to select elderly hosts due to their slow pace, making them easier to stalk. Children are much too fast for the cucumbersome, which is a shame since they're an endless source of muck.

Many elderly people have suffered fractures when tripping on a sticky cucumbersome. For unknown reasons, domestic cats (*Felis silvestris catus*) detest the cucumbersome. One hypothesis is that their hatred stems from the many hospitalizations this animal causes the older population, leading to kitties not receiving their kibble in a timely fashion.

*Fig. 1* A TYPICAL CUCUMBERSOME ACCIDENT

PLATE **XXVII**

# THE
# BEARDED DESERT
# SLURPETTER

Attentive ears

Unassuming stare

Always well-groomed

Normal back

Massive tongue (obviously we can't see it right now)

Snazzy little beard

Varied colors: from sandy brown to sandy beige

Prehensile paws

Tail that always touches the ground

Weight: 52 kg (12 of which are tongue)
114.6 lb (26.4 of which are tongue)

**DISTINGUISHING FEATURE**
It has the longest tongue of any animal in the world (proportionally to its body, of course).

**SIZE**
4 m / 13 ft

**HABITAT**
Deserts, beaches, sandboxes

PLATE XXVIII

This friendly animal has one very bad habit: while eating, the slurpetter makes a terrible noise due to its enormous tongue. In its defense, it holds its spoon correctly thanks to its five-fingered paws, it uses its serviette properly, it does not lean over its plate too much, and it knows the difference between the fish knife and the cheese knife. However, it does slurp its soup, chew with its mouth open, suck the meat off bones, talk with its mouth full, and glug-glug-glug when it drinks. It is truly unbearable!

As a result, the desert nomads avoid it* like the plague, since sharing a meal with a slurpetter takes incredible composure. These desert nomads, known as the Tuaregs, are well-versed in the art of keeping cool and hydrated. They also wear blue scarves over their noses to protect themselves from spit, should they come across a slurpetter during their travels. In any event, the desert remains the desert, and what will be will be.

*Fig. 1* SLURPETTERS AND THEIR TONGUE-IN-CHEEK HUMOR

* This is easy to do, as its tail leaves a telltale trail in the sand.

PLATE XXIX

# THE
# MUSHACORN

Not-the-least-bit-
sharp horn

Unblemished
baboon-like snout

Well-groomed
and exuberant tail

Super clean fur
with nice little curls

Impeccably
hairless legs

Weight: 10 kg / 22 lb*

**DISTINGUISHING FEATURE**
Diet uniquely comprised of
Rafflesia arnoldii (the world's
largest flower)

**HORN LENGTH**
13.5 cm / 5.3 in

**BODY LENGTH***
100 cm / 39.4 in

**HABITAT**
Indonesian forests

* Exactly like the *Rafflesia arnoldii*

PLATE **XXX**

The mushacorn is a relatively uninteresting specimen. The Indonesian people call it the "kuda titi," which makes it giggle. Contrary to the horns of the unicorn or the rhinoceros, which are said to have magical properties, the mushacorn's horn is simply a fleshy protrusion — likely a wart. The mushacorn is impeccably clean and spends most of its day grooming. Like the domestic cat, it can spend hours licking its own posterior, which is, simply put, disgusting. In the case of cats, they are at least adorable and sweet, unlike the mushacorn. Thanks to its useless horn and its toxic flesh, the mushacorn is not in any danger of becoming extinct. In short, it leads a good life.

It is rumored that a number of Indonesians believe its horn is not a horn, but something else entirely. Decency prevents me from elaborating on this preposterous theory.

*Fig. 1* MUSHACORNS GROOMING

# The Not-useless
# Animals

PLATE **XXXI**

# THE
# SLIGGLE

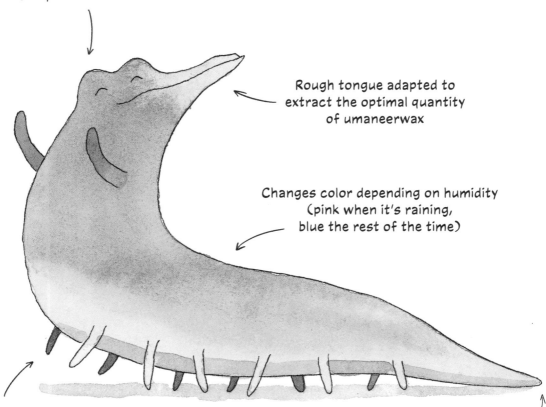

Complete lack of ears

Rough tongue adapted to extract the optimal quantity of umaneerwax

Changes color depending on humidity (pink when it's raining, blue the rest of the time)

Seven pairs of legs, 14 legs total

Blunt extremities to avoid auricular injuries

**DISTINGUISHING FEATURES**
Can keep a beat.

Knows how to give massages.

Only eats flower pistils.

**LENGTH**
The finest specimens are 6 cm (2.4 in).

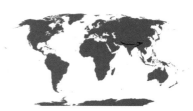

**HABITAT**
The mountains of Zhangjiajie National Park (like the castinnitus)

PLATE **XXXII**

This little land mollusk resembles a slug that wiggles (hence its well-appointed name). Unlike the slug, the sliggle has seven pairs of tiny legs that allow it to interpret many difficult dance moves. Unfortunately, it is much too small to participate in dance competitions, which is unfortunate. Let's be honest, though: who wants to watch a dancing slug when one can watch kittens in tutus on the Internet? Thankfully, the sliggle has no interest in social media or stardom. In all likelihood, as you read this, it is happily spending its days dancing a lindy hop under the shade of a mandarin tree.

The sliggle has many other rewarding uses. Mollusk or not, they are a proud species…

Put it in an ear and it protects from the song of the castinnitus.

Set it under a nose and it makes for a dapper mustache.

It also makes an original utensil-rest for the holidays.

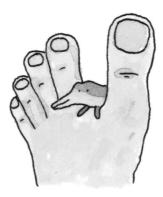
Used between toes, it's perfect for pedicure enthusiasts.

Glued to a seashell, it becomes a handy barometer, perfect for Mother's Day.

*Fig. 1* THE MANY USES OF THE SLIGGLE IN A HUMAN'S EVERYDAY LIFE

PLATE **XXXIII**

# THE
# JAPANESE PERUKE

Thick coat resembling
the finest toupees

Tiny, sparkling eyes
(if you can find them)

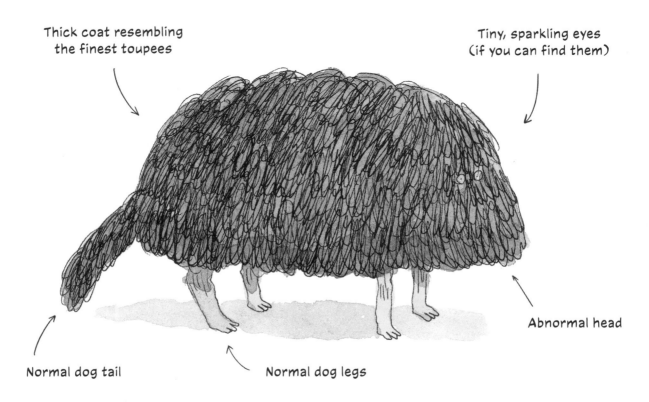

Normal dog tail

Normal dog legs

Abnormal head

Weight when dry:
5 kg (11 lb)

Weight when wet:
5 kg (11 lb)

**DISTINGUISHING FEATURE**
It does not bark (its cousin, the
Akita Inu, is not a very vocal dog
either, but at least it has a head).

**SIZE**
105 cm / 41.3 in

**HABITAT**
Japan, Perukashima Island

PLATE **XXXIV**

The Japanese Peruke (*Canis impermeablus*) is no ordinary dog — it has no head, after all. However, it does have a tail, which has helped the world's leading scientists distinguish its front from its rear. These same scientists have long wondered if this creature has a specific purpose. Its use was discovered accidentally* by one of the laboratories' cleaning people when they tried to mop up the floor with one of these dogs: it turns out that the Japanese Peruke isn't the least bit absorbent. This incredible property actually has many practical uses in everyday life. When thrown in a pool, the peruke does not make the water level go down. It stays dry in the rain. When exiting a river, it shakes itself off without splashing anyone. It is brilliant when skipped across a lake. And, lastly, it never needs a bath, which is the ultimate goal of any self-respecting dog.

*Fig. 1* **THE PERUKE IS FAMOUS IN JAPANESE ART.**

* That's what we call "serendipitous".

PLATE **XXXV**

# THE
# SHENANIPOOCH

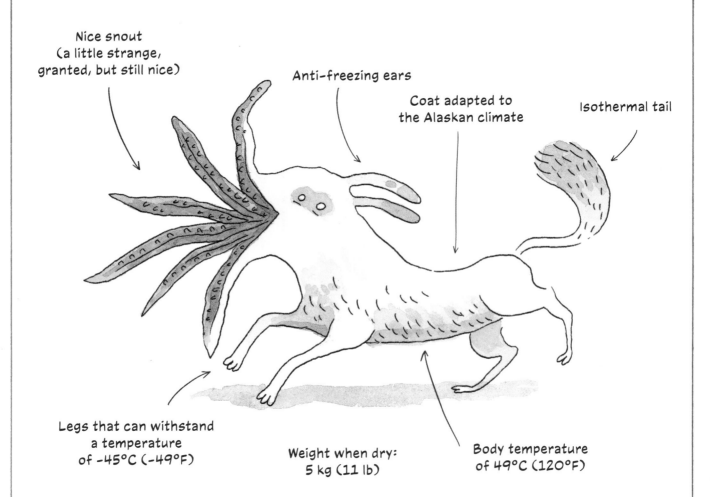

Nice snout
(a little strange,
granted, but still nice)

Anti-freezing ears

Coat adapted to
the Alaskan climate

Isothermal tail

Legs that can withstand
a temperature
of -45°C (-49°F)

Weight when dry:
5 kg (11 lb)

Body temperature
of 49°C (120°F)

**DISTINGUISHING FEATURES**
Shakes its tail in a figure-eight motion.

Is scared of bananas.

Eats all the kibble, even the veggie ones.

**SIZE**
61 cm / 24 in
(like a giant chihuahua)

**HABITAT**
Alaska's western coast,
on the shores on the Boring Sea

PLATE **XXXVI**

The shenanipooch is also a close cousin to the dog, with the exception of its very peculiar snout. Like all dogs, it wags its tail, drools on the sofa, drinks from the toilet, and chases seals (there are no cats on the shores of the Boring Sea). That's all well and good, but it's not very useful. What *is* useful is the shenanipooch's endless repertoire of witty jokes. Unlike some humans*, it never tells the same joke twice. The shenanipooch is the life of the party, side-splittingly funny and refined. The only issue? If two shenanipooches are together in a room, they will tell each other jokes until they die laughing or from exhaustion. The shenanipooch is highly sought after by their human neighbors because, to be honest, when the 11-month-long winter settles on the shores of the Boring Sea, things can get quite grim.

*Fig. 1* IN THE VET'S WAITING ROOM

* My cousin Nigel, for example, who can be such a bore.

# The Not-friendly Animals

PLATE XXXVII

# THE
# GRUMP MITE

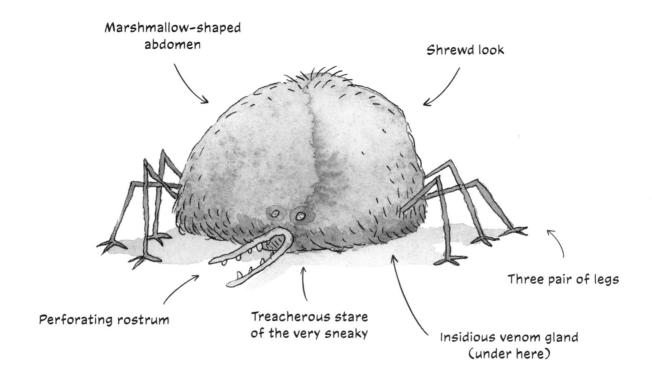

Marshmallow-shaped
abdomen

Shrewd look

Perforating rostrum

Treacherous stare
of the very sneaky

Three pair of legs

Insidious venom gland
(under here)

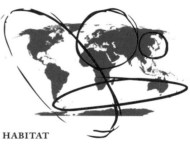

**DISTINGUISHING FEATURE**
Unlike other mites, the grump
mite has only six legs.

**SIZE**
3.2 nm / 1.2598e-7 in

**HABITAT**
Absolutely everywhere on Earth

PLATE XXXVIII

Invisible to the naked eye, this mite has a gift for ruining the ambiance, spoiling the atmosphere, and generally wrecking the day. Its sting contains venom that changes the mood of post-pubescent* humans (that is to say, adults). When stung, they become irritated; yell about putting away the dishes; complain that, in their day, people didn't do homework at the last minute on Sunday evenings; and confiscate electronic devices while ranting about what this godforsaken world is coming to. The only known antidote to the grump mite's bite is the "kissy for my darling daddy" or "lovely mumsy" — but, let's be honest, nobody wants to kiss vociferating and expectorating post-pubescents.

*Fig. 1* BITTEN ADULT RECEIVING THE ANTIDOTE

* Covered in hair, shaved or otherwise

PLATE **XXXIX**

# THE
# DACHSHEPHANT

Looks like an annoying
pain in the neck

Floppy ears

Thick, damp skin
that smells of plasticine

Humdrum
tail

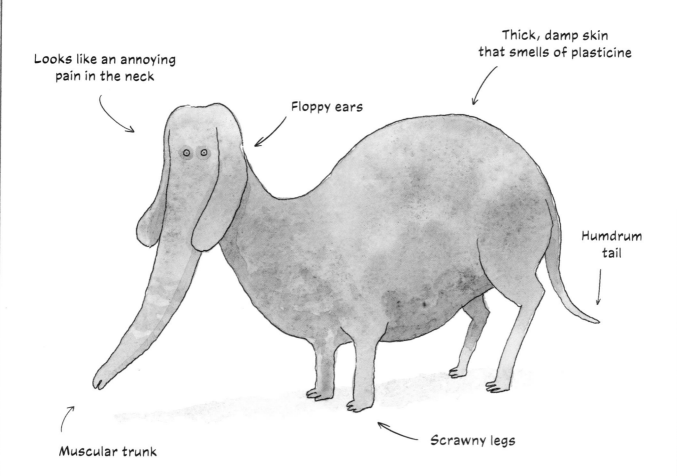

Muscular trunk

Scrawny legs

**DISTINGUISHING FEATURES**
Is a first-rate grouch.

Enjoys political TV shows.

Can do the moonwalk.

**TRUNK LENGTH**
2 m / 6.5 ft

**HEIGHT**
2 m / 6.5 ft

**BODY LENGTH**
4.3 m / 14.1 ft

**HABITAT**
Anywhere there are green things
to eat

PLATE XL

Certain scientists believe that the dachshephant is a pachyderm, while others believe it isn't. This grouchy animal is extremely picky: it will only eat green things, hence its color. Salad, frogs, parsley, pistachio paste, kiwis, clover, leprechauns, parakeets, kale shakes… anything green, no matter how gross. If offered something that is another color, the enormous beast growls and has a tantrum, breaking everything with its phenomenally strong trunk*. Whatever you do, never ever give it beige food, as it will explode. Literally. There will be pieces of dachshephant in every nook and cranny, and you will have to do a full day of laundry. Extremely rare, the colorblind dachshephant is even harder to contend with. Avoid crossing its path at all cost.

*Fig. 1* SCIENTISTS EXPERIMENTING WITH THE INGESTION OF CHICKPEAS BY A BLINDFOLDED ADULT MALE DACHSHEPHANT

* It doesn't look like much here, I know.

# 8

# The Now-flightless Animals

PLATE XLI

# THE
# ANGORA CASSOWARY

Incredible hearing

Distinguished nuptial parade crest

360° vision

Puny wings (from having never been used)

Premium-quality feathers

High-precision beak

**DISTINGUISHING FEATURES**
Knows all multiples of 17 by heart.

Never cleans its nest.

Brushes its beak when pigs fly.

**WING LENGTH**
3 cm / 1.2 in

**BODY LENGTH**
9 cm / 3.5 in

**HABITAT**
The groves of Upper Karabakh

PLATE XLII

The Angora cassowary is a bird, but it does not fly. It could fly, but it doesn't feel like it. It prefers to stay in its nest and wait for insects to come to it before eating. It also doesn't leave its nest to find a mate, which is fine since it doesn't have the patience to brood any eggs. Brooding is too tedious a task for the Angora cassowary. It might stretch its wings to fan itself on very hot days, but that's about it. It does know its multiples of 17 by heart, which comes in handy when calculating its feathers or counting the leaves on trees when it inevitably gets bored. In short, the Angora cassowary is not a very interesting creature, in spite of its angora feathers — and, even then, only if you like indigo.

An Angora cassowary was once observed out of its nest, but the specimen was simply sleepwalking.

*Fig. 1* THE FIRST (AND LAST) FLYING ANGORA CASSOWARY

PLATE XLIII

# THE
# GALLUS GALLUS GALLUS

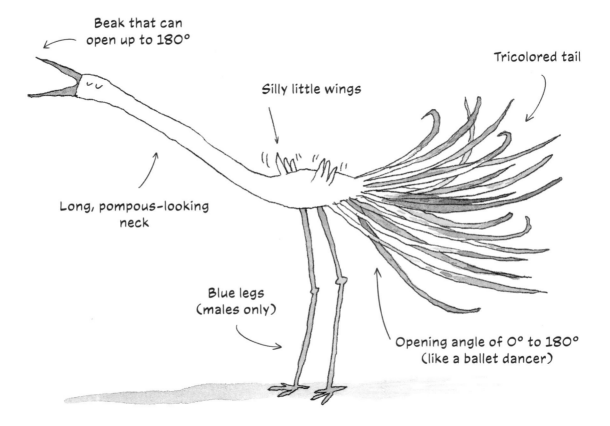

Beak that can open up to 180°

Silly little wings

Tricolored tail

Long, pompous-looking neck

Blue legs (males only)

Opening angle of 0° to 180° (like a ballet dancer)

**DISTINGUISHING FEATURES**
Loves baguettes.

Is a sore loser.

Is terrible at pétanque.

**SIZE**
1.10 m / 3.6 ft

**HABITAT**
Lives exclusively in the tiny village of Nojals-et-Clotte (Dordogne, France).

PLATE XLIV

Commonly referred to as the "venerable rooster" (cousin of the domestic rooster), the gallus gallus gallus refuses to fly. It considers the act generally intolerable and, frankly, you'd have to pay it more (or anything at all) to fly. It's on flight strike! Admittedly, flying would be difficult with such small wings. Endowed with a beautiful panache and a powerful voice, it parades in flocks to reclaim its right not to fly, to defend the rights of all gallinaceous birds, and denounce the fowl living conditions of foul*. Thanks to its long neck, it can swallow a baguette whole, which is splendid since it could not carry a baguette home under one of its tiny wings, a required practice throughout France.

The expression "the rooster may crow, but the hen lays the eggs" is incorrect in the case of the gallus gallus gallus. In this species, the male also lays the eggs, while the female does other things.

*Fig. 1* A WOLF HUNTING A GALLUS GALLUS GALLUS

* Or maybe it's the other way around?

PLATE **XLV**

# THE
# SNUROBOROS

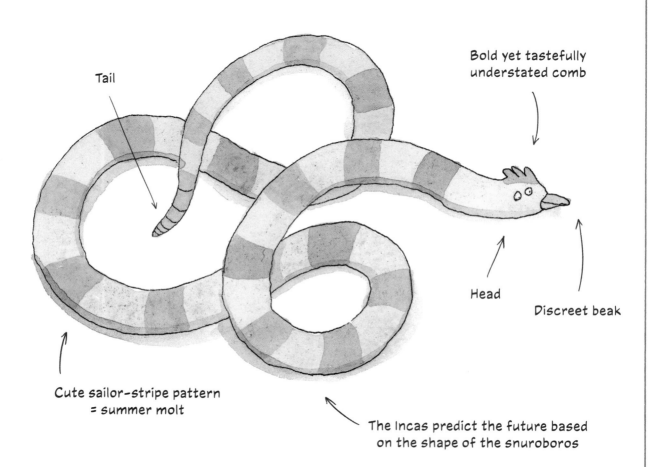

Tail

Bold yet tastefully
understated comb

Head

Discreet beak

Cute sailor-stripe pattern
= summer molt

The Incas predict the future based
on the shape of the snuroboros

**DISTINGUISHING FEATURES**

Changes pattern with every molt.

Enjoys annoying the Incas
by tying itself in knots.

Claims to be "everything and
nothing" at the same time.

**LENGTH**
Sometimes short, sometimes long,
but mostly long enough

**HABITAT**
Mountains of Bolivia

PLATE XLVI

The snuroboros is the only bird with scales in all of creation. Moreover, like other birds, it has no arms. It also has no wings, flying instead by propelling itself into the air like a spring. Rather than listing everything it doesn't have, it would be easier to talk about what it does have: a head and a tail.

Fortunately, the snuroboros makes the most of its small cranial capacity. It has an exceptional memory and can remember absolutely everything: the exact date and time when it molted into a pink and yellow polka-dotted pattern, the number of blades of grass in the clearing, the maiden name of its great-grandmother's half-sister's second cousin… Also, the rattle at the end of its tail makes no noise. It's just for show.

The snuroboros has unending growth. It feeds on itself, which is quite practical. The expression "full circle" was inspired by the snuroboros. It means that the circle is complete and that we can move on to other things.

*Fig. 1* FUNNY MIX-UP BETWEEN TWO SNUROBOROS
(INTERPRETED AS THE END OF THE WORLD BY THE INCAS)

# 9

## The Shifty Animals

PLATE XLVII

# THE
# RICK O'REY AMOEBA

Vibratile cilia

Cytoplasmic liquid

Nucleus

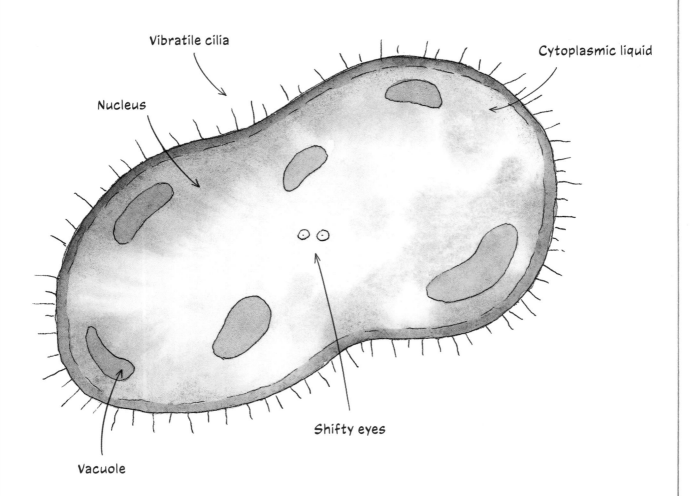

Shifty eyes

Vacuole

**DISTINGUISHING FEATURES**
Nothing really…

Its ability to reproduce itself
at will, maybe?

Or its ability to withstand
freezing?

**CIRCUMFERENCE**
0.0087 mm / 0.0003 in

**HABITAT**
Puddles, dog bowls, kiddy pools

PLATE XLVIII

What can be said about the Rick O'Rey amoeba? Not much, actually. It is a simple protozoan that does nothing except marinate in stagnant and brackish water, the primordial soup of all life on Earth. The amoeba wiggles its vibratile cilia (miniscule eyelash-like hairs) to move around its puddle. Sometimes, it splits itself in half and, voilà, there are two. That about covers it, though. The amoeba is not shifty per se, but it does have a shifty look. That's why the editorial committee agreed to include it in this chapter.

This amoeba was discovered by my colleague and friend Rick O'Rey, which is why it bears his name. He brought it back with him during a trip to Papua by ingesting a dubious drink. It is not one of his fondest travel memories…

"Cheers" means "dishwater" in ancient Papuan.

*Fig. 1* RICK O'REY DISCOVERING THE FAMOUS AMOEBA OF THE SAME NAME

PLATE XLIX

# THE
# IZANEEWANEER

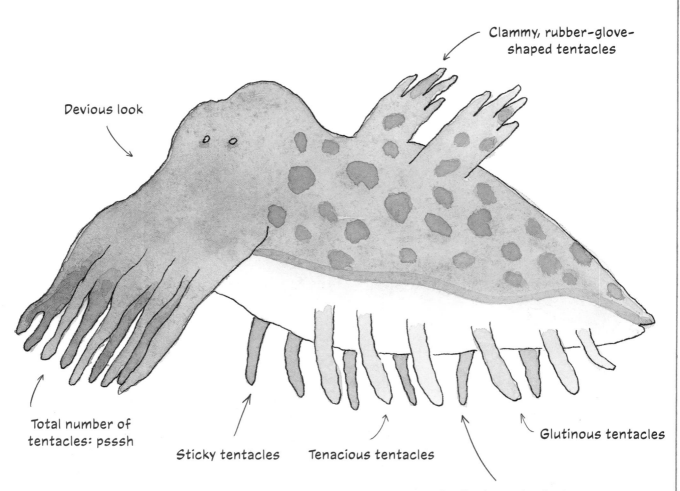

Clammy, rubber-glove-shaped tentacles

Devious look

Total number of tentacles: psssh

Sticky tentacles

Tenacious tentacles

Glutinous tentacles

Mucilaginous tentacles

**DISTINGUISHING FEATURE**
Where do I start? Everything is odd with this one.

**SIZE**
15 cm / 5.9 in

**HABITAT**
Seafloor and supermarket air vents

PLATE L

The izaneewaneer is shifty. Shifty, shifty, shifty! So shifty, in fact, that no scientist has ever attempted to study it. Tentacles on its head, tentacles on its body, tentacles on its back: safe to say, this does not make for a cuddly animal. One could even say it is quite revolting. For all we know, the izaneewaneer could be convivial, funny, and affectionate. It might even smell good and taste even better. But no one will ever know because of how shifty, devious, and cagey it looks. There! I said it! Even among themselves, the izaneewaneers find each other untrustworthy, which makes for a very sad and solitary life.

*Fig. 1* A SAD, SOLITARY SPECIMEN SEARCHING
THE USUALLY LIVELY SEAFLOOR FOR A FRIEND

PLATE LI

# THE
# BIZARD

Head 1

Different pattern from the other head

Beautiful keratinous comb

Head 2

As you can see, very different

Opposite-facing legs, which make walking a challenge

**DISTINGUISHING FEATURES**
Continuously changes its accent.

Loves ping-pong and tennis, and can watch an entire match without turning its head.

**HEAD I HEIGHT**
1.1 m / 3.6 ft

**HEAD 2 HEIGHT**
1.2 m / 3.9 ft

**HABITAT**
Flemish plains

PLATE LII

The bizard is always saying everything and its opposite. It cannot be trusted. It doesn't even know which way to go. In short, it is bipolar. Some specimens are even tripolar. One solution could be to cut them in half, but that would be quite wasteful and, frankly, it's not a very nice thing to do. Its diet is extremely complicated in that one side of the bizard is vegan and the other is not. This results in epic arguments. Apart from that, it can make for nice company if one enjoys endless discussions or even listening to it talking to itself for hours while imitating your accent (best not to be easily offended). Also, it is a master of hide-and-seek: while one head counts facing a tree, the other can sneak a peek at hiding spots. Lastly, the bizard is not that shifty, but it is shifty enough to warrant inclusion in this chapter.

*Fig. 1* **A TYPICAL BIZARD MONOLOGUE**

# AFTERWORD

Regrettably, this enlightening document is incomplete, as evidenced by the last page of the professor's journal. Still, we felt that it deserved this beautiful, limited-edition printing in the interest of honoring his memory and enriching the international scientific heritage of his exceptional knowledge. This last page, ripped from the journal and found between the toes of the Statue of Liberty, covered in lasagna stains and badly battered, was restored and decrypted by a world-renowned graphologist. Shown opposite is the transcription.